Washington Avenue Branch
Albany Public Library

APR 2 6 2016

W9-BCO-653

Jack's Worry

Sam Zuppardi

CANDLEWICK PRESS

Jack loved playing
the trumpet.

For weeks, he had been looking forward to playing for his mom in his first-ever concert.

But on the morning of the big day,
he found he had a Worry.

"Time to get up," said Jack's mom. "I've made you a special pre-concert breakfast."

Jack crawled under
the blankets.
But his Worry crawled
under with him.

Jack hid under the bed.
But his Worry followed
him there, too.

When Jack finally got downstairs, his Worry made it hard for him to eat his special breakfast.

"Everything OK?" asked his mom.

Jack wanted to tell her about his Worry,
but he couldn't find the words.

After breakfast, Jack ran around the yard, trying to lose his Worry.

But every time he
stopped, it caught right
back up with him.

So Jack did the one thing that always made him happy. . . .

He took out his trumpet
and started to play.

But that only made things worse.

Jack's Worry was here to stay.

"It's almost time to go," Jack's mom said.

But Jack couldn't go to the concert with such a big Worry.

He couldn't do anything with such a big Worry.

Suddenly, it was all a bit too much for Jack.

Jack's mom crouched in front of him.
"I thought you were looking forward
to today," she said.

For the first time that day,
Jack stopped trying to get rid
of his Worry. Instead, he looked
at it. Really looked at it.

And he found
the words he needed.

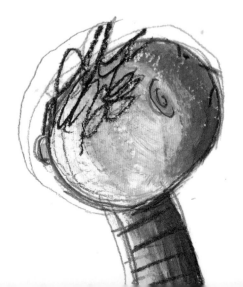

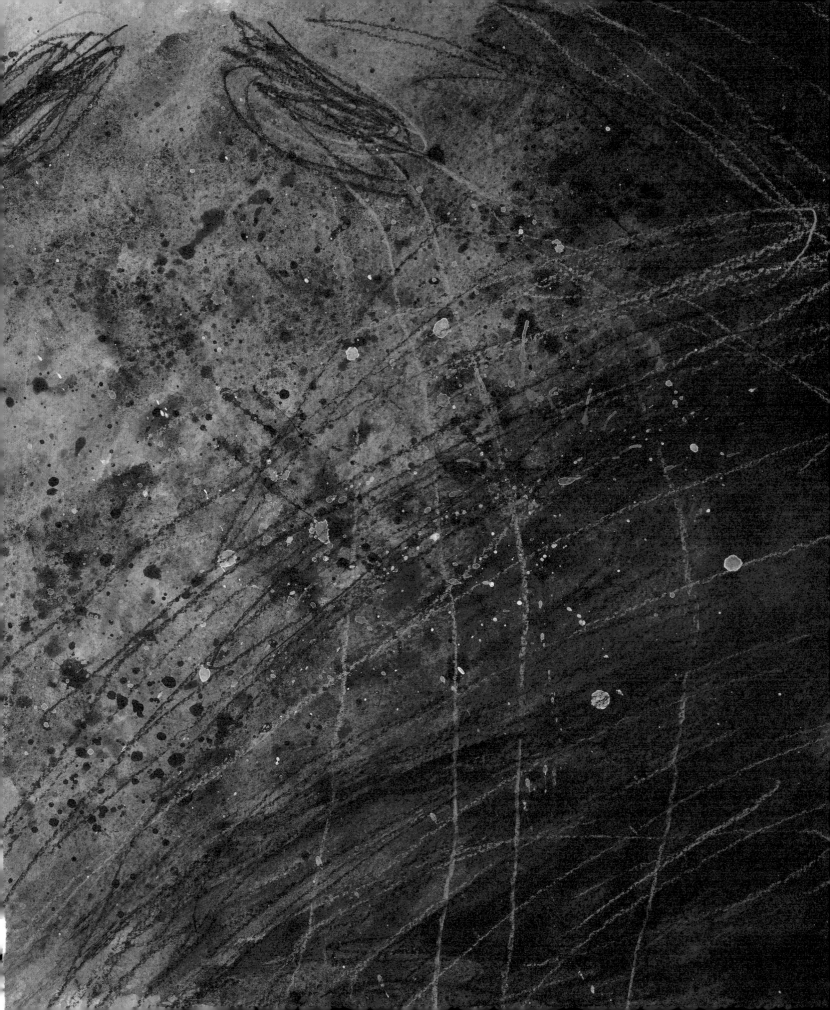

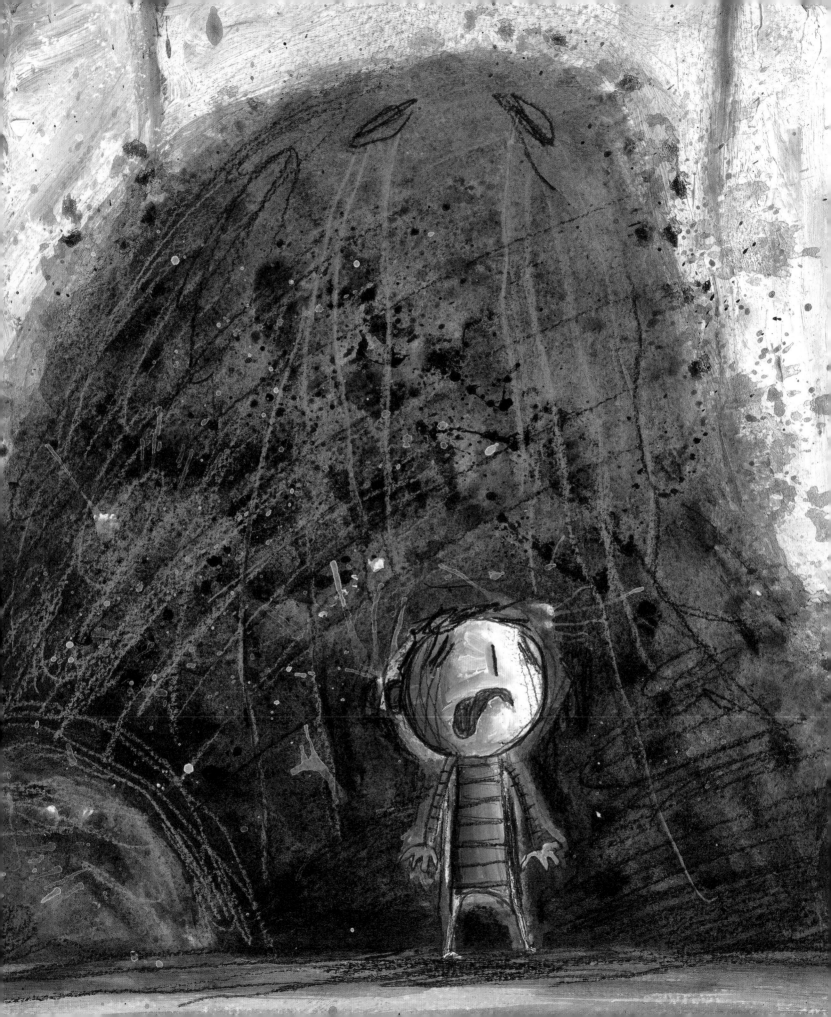

"I don't want to play in the concert!"
he told his mom.
"I'm worried I'll make a mistake
and you won't love me anymore!"

"That's quite a worry," said Jack's mom.
"I'm glad you told me. And you know what?
The concert isn't about playing perfectly.
It's about having fun, and sharing something
you love with people who love you.

And I will still
love you even if
you play every
note wrong."

Suddenly Jack's Worry
wasn't so big anymore.

By the time they got to the school, his Worry was teeny-tiny.

When he saw his friends with their Worries, he knew just what to do.

And the mistakes? There were a few—
but Jack was too busy enjoying
himself to worry.

For Luisa

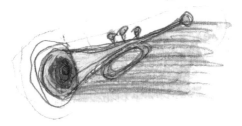

Copyright © 2016 by Sam Zuppardi

All rights reserved. No part of this book may be reproduced, transmitted, or stored in an information retrieval system in any form or by any means, graphic, electronic, or mechanical, including photocopying, taping, and recording, without prior written permission from the publisher.

First edition 2016

Library of Congress Catalog Card Number 2015934266
ISBN 978-0-7636-7845-6

16 17 18 19 20 21 CCP 10 9 8 7 6 5 4 3 2 1

Printed in Shenzhen, Guangdong, China

This book was typeset in Schoolbell.
The illustrations were done in acrylic paint and pencil on watercolor paper.

Candlewick Press
99 Dover Street
Somerville, Massachusetts 02144

visit us at www.candlewick.com